Beatrix Potter

The Tale of
Peter Rabbit

Illustrated by
Michael Hague

SeaStar Books • New York

SEASTAR BOOKS
A division of NORTH-SOUTH BOOKS INC.

First published in the United States by SeaStar Books,
a division of North-South Books Inc., New York. Published simultaneously in Canada by
North-South Books, an imprint of Nord-Süd Verlag AG, Gossau Zürich, Switzerland.

Library of Congress Cataloging-in-Publication Data
Potter, Beatrix, 1866–1943.
The tale of Peter Rabbit / by Beatrix Potter; illustrated by Michael Hague.
p.   cm.
Summary: Peter disobeys his mother by going into Mr. McGregor's garden and almost gets caught.
[1. Rabbits—Fiction.]   I. Hague, Michael, ill.   II. Title.
PZ7.P85 Tap 2001
[E]—dc21   00-10433

The art for this book was prepared using pen and ink, watercolor, and colored pencils.
The text for this book is set in 17-point Colwell.

ISBN 1-58717-052-3 (trade binding)
1 3 5 7 9 TB 10 8 6 4 2
ISBN 1-58717-053-1 (library binding)
1 3 5 7 9 LB 10 8 6 4 2

Printed in Hong Kong by South China Printing Company (1988) Ltd.

For more information about our books, and the authors and artists who create them,
visit our web site: www.northsouth.com

To Kathleen

Once upon a time there were four little Rabbits, and
their names were—Flopsy, Mopsy, Cotton-tail, and Peter.
They lived with their Mother in a sand-bank, underneath
the root of a very big fir-tree.

"Now, my dears," said old Mrs. Rabbit one morning, "you may go into the fields or down the lane, but don't go into Mr. McGregor's garden: your Father had an accident there; he was put in a pie by Mrs. McGregor.

"Now run along, and don't get into mischief. I am going out."

Then old Mrs. Rabbit took a basket and her umbrella, and went through the wood to the baker's. She bought a loaf of brown bread and five currant buns.

Flopsy, Mopsy, and Cotton-tail, who were good little bunnies,
went down the lane to gather blackberries.

But Peter, who was very naughty, ran straight away to
Mr. McGregor's garden, and squeezed under the gate!

First he ate some lettuces and some French beans; and then
he ate some radishes;

And then, feeling rather sick, he went to look for some
parsley.

But round the end of a cucumber frame, whom should
he meet but Mr. McGregor!

Mr. McGregor was on his hands and knees planting out young cabbages, but he jumped up and ran after Peter, waving a rake and calling out,

"Stop thief!"

Peter was most dreadfully frightened; he rushed all over the garden, for he had forgotten the way back to the gate.

He lost one of his shoes among the cabbages, and the other shoe amongst the potatoes.

After losing them, he ran on four legs and went faster, so
that I think he might have got away altogether if he had
not unfortunately run into a gooseberry net, and got caught
by the large buttons on his jacket. It was a blue jacket
with brass buttons, quite new.

Peter gave himself up for lost, and shed big tears; but his sobs were overheard by some friendly sparrows, who flew to him in great excitement, and implored him to exert himself.

Mr. McGregor came up with a sieve, which he intended to pop upon the top of Peter; but Peter wriggled out just in time, leaving his jacket behind him.

And rushed into the tool-shed, and jumped into a can. It would have been a beautiful thing to hide in, if it had not had so much water in it.

Mr. McGregor was quite sure that Peter was somewhere in the tool-shed, perhaps hidden underneath a flower-pot. He began to turn them over carefully, looking under each.

Presently Peter sneezed—"*Kertyschoo!*" Mr. McGregor was after him in no time.

And tried to put his foot upon Peter, who jumped out of a window, upsetting three plants. The window was too small for Mr. McGregor, and he was tired of running after Peter. He went back to his work.

Peter sat down to rest; he was out of breath and trembling
with fright, and he had not the least idea which way to go.
Also he was very damp with sitting in that can.

After a time he began to wander about, going
lippity—lippity—not very fast, and looking all round.

He found a door in a wall; but it was locked, and there was no room for a fat little rabbit to squeeze underneath.

An old mouse was running in and out over the stone door-step, carrying peas and beans to her family in the wood. Peter asked her the way to the gate, but she had such a large pea in her mouth that she could not answer. She only shook her head at him. Peter began to cry.

Then he tried to find his way straight across the garden,
but he became more and more puzzled. Presently, he came
to a pond where Mr. McGregor filled his water-cans. A
cat was staring at some gold-fish; she sat very, very still, but
now and then the tip of her tail twitched as if it were alive.
Peter thought it best to go away without speaking to her; he
had heard about cats from his cousin, little Benjamin Bunny.

He went back towards the tool-shed, but suddenly, quite close
to him, he heard the noise of a hoe—*scr-r-ritch*, *scratch*,
scratch, *scritch*. Peter scuttered underneath the bushes.

But presently, as nothing happened, he came out, and climbed
upon a wheelbarrow and peeped over. The first thing he saw
was Mr. McGregor hoeing onions. His back was turned
towards Peter, and beyond him was the gate!

Peter got down very quietly off the wheelbarrow, and started running as fast as he could go, along a straight walk behind some black-currant bushes.

Mr. McGregor caught sight of him at the corner, but Peter did not care. He slipped underneath the gate,

and was safe at last in the wood outside the garden.

Mr. McGregor hung up the little jacket and the shoes for a scare-crow to frighten the blackbirds.

Peter never stopped running or looked behind him till he got home to the big fir-tree.

He was so tired that he flopped down upon the nice soft sand on the floor of the rabbit-hole and shut his eyes. His mother was busy cooking; she wondered what he had done with his clothes. It was the second little jacket and pair of shoes that Peter had lost in a fortnight!

I am sorry to say that Peter was not very well during the evening. His mother put him to bed, and made some camomile tea; and she gave a dose of it to Peter!

"One table-spoonful to be taken at bed-time."

But Flopsy, Mopsy, and Cotton-tail had bread and milk and blackberries for supper.